An I Can Read Book™

ADVENTURES OF

Sandy Creek

TRANSFORMERS™

MEET THE AUTOBOTS

Adapted by Jennifer Frantz
Illustrations by Guido Guidi
Based on the Screenplay by Roberto Orci & Alex
Kurtzman from a Story by Roberto Orci & Alex Kurtzman
and John Rogers

The Autobots are Transformers.

They fight for good and freedom.

Their planet, Cybertron,

was destroyed in a battle

with the evil Decepticons.

Now they have landed on Earth!

The Autobots are searching
for a new home.
They are also looking
for something else. . . .

MISSION

To find the Allspark,
the core of all robot life force,
before the Decepticons do.

Bumblebee gets a cool new shape, too!

Bumblebee is happy

when his friend Sam smiles.

But danger is just around the corner.

This is not a real cop on patrol!

Bumblebee transforms

into a supersonic bad-guy blaster.

With a fast move,

he saves his human pals

from a deadly Decepticon.

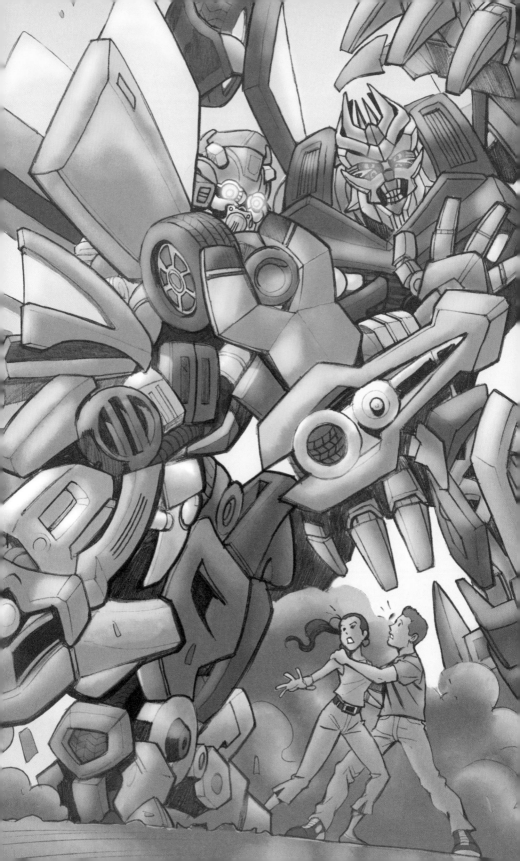

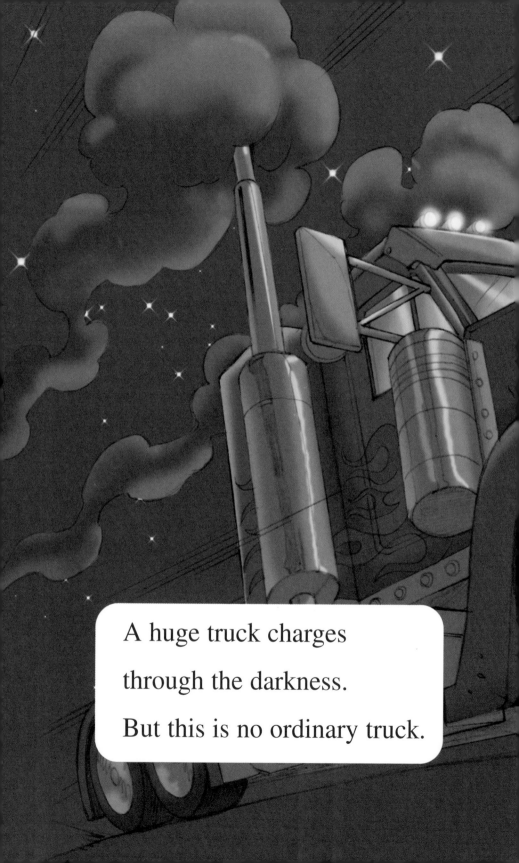

A huge truck charges
through the darkness.
But this is no ordinary truck.

It is Optimus Prime—
leader of the Autobots!
He is strong and good.
Optimus Prime calls
his Autobot friends.

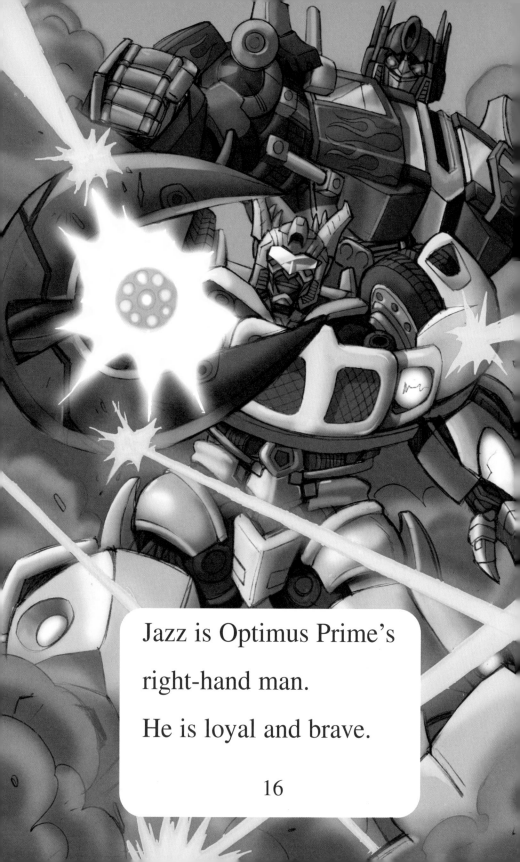

Jazz is Optimus Prime's
right-hand man.
He is loyal and brave.

16

No one can top Jazz's speed and style.

Ironhide knows all about fighting.

He is one tough Autobot!

He's always ready to blast
his way out of danger.

19

Ratchet can see trouble

a mile away.

He has X-ray vision!

Ratchet is the rescue truck.

He is always there to help a friend.

"Autobots: Roll out!"

Optimus Prime orders.

It's time to find the Allspark
and stop the evil Decepticons.

Yikes! The Autobots are trapped.

But it's nothing a powerful pulse blast

can't handle!

Using a little teamwork,
they get rid of the threat.

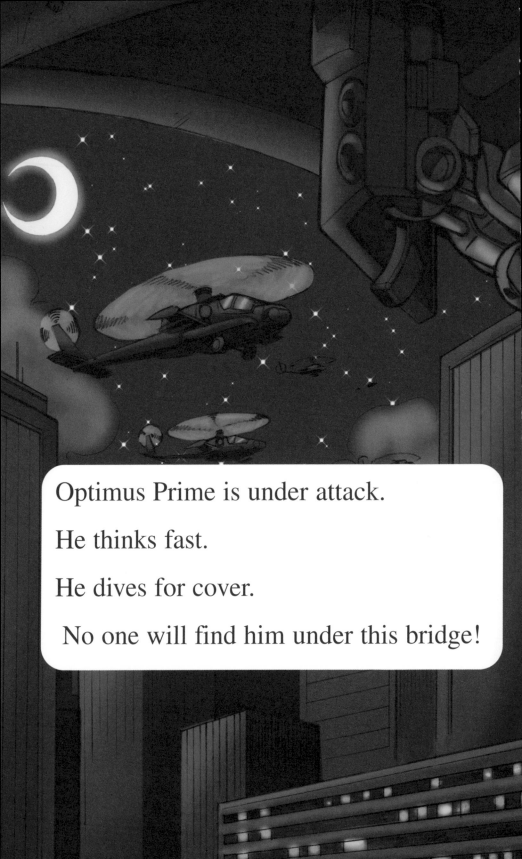

Optimus Prime is under attack.

He thinks fast.

He dives for cover.

No one will find him under this bridge!

The Autobots battle the Decepticons

for the Allspark.

Bumblebee takes a bad hit,

but he will be okay.

Optimus Prime swoops in to save Sam.

And Sam saves the Allspark!

Optimus Prime fights to the end.

Optimus Prime and the Autobots have saved Earth. In return, the Autobots have a new planet to call home.

They will live on Earth—

hidden safely in the human world.

Optimus Prime stands quietly.

Life is good, he thinks.

TRANS FORMERS ™

MEET THE DECEPTICONS

Adapted by Jennifer Frantz
Illustrations by Guido Guidi
Based on the Screenplay by Roberto Orci & Alex
Kurtzman from a Story by Roberto Orci & Alex Kurtzman
and John Rogers

Evil alien robots called Decepticons
have landed on Earth.
They are from the planet Cybertron.

37

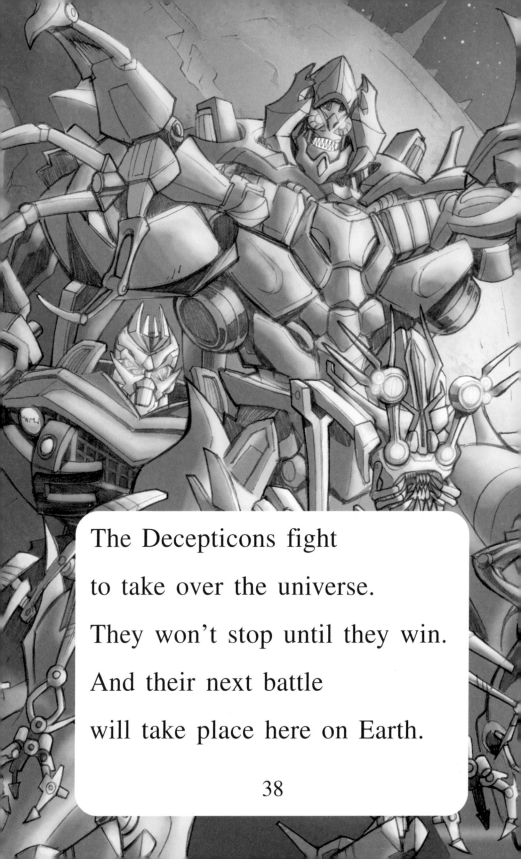

The Decepticons fight
to take over the universe.
They won't stop until they win.
And their next battle
will take place here on Earth.

38

The Decepticons are Transformers.

They are robots that hide among us.

They pretend to be regular machines.

They are very tricky and very bad.

41

A friendly chopper comes in for a landing.

But that chopper isn't what it seems.

It turns into a Decepticon named Blackout!

Blackout crushes steel cars.

His blasts wipe out anything in his way.

Blackout is full of nasty surprises.

He carries a robot named Skorponok.

Skorponok digs through the desert sand.

He can sense anything that moves.

He hunts like a scorpion.

He is dangerous.

Frenzy is a Decepticon, too.

He is very tricky.

He can turn into a radio or a boom box.

When he is a robot,

he can shoot metal discs.

Frenzy wants to make big trouble.
He shuts down all the computers
with his terrible scream.

Barricade is another bad guy.

He can transform into a police car.

Frenzy wants to come along.

He turns into the car's CD player.

They drive the streets
looking for trouble.

Megatron is the most powerful

of all Decepticons.

He is a metal giant.

He feeds on energy.

Megatron won't rest

until he finds the Allspark.

It is the Transformers' life force.

Megatron wants it all for himself!

Megatron transforms into

a supersonic jet.

He blasts off on his evil mission.

Megatron finds what he is looking for.

It's the Allspark!

He sends a signal

to the other Decepticons.

Decepticons come
from all over
to help their leader.
The Decepticon named Starscream
jets through the sky.

Bonecrusher and Brawl

rumble over the ground.

The Decepticons unite.

Blackout

Skorponok

Barricade

Frenzy

Together they are a deadly force.

Starscream

Bonecrusher

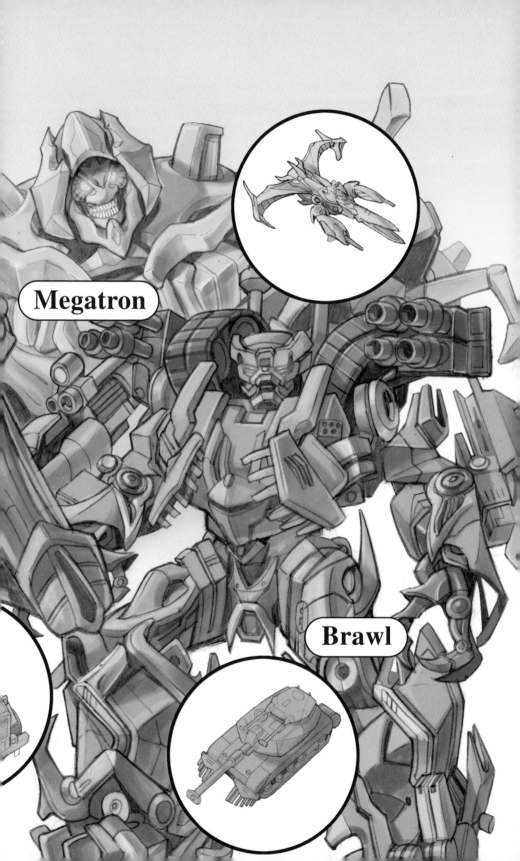

Who can stop Megatron
and his Decepticon army?
The Autobots!

Autobots are good Transformers.

Their leader is Optimus Prime.

They want to save Earth

from the evil Decepticons.

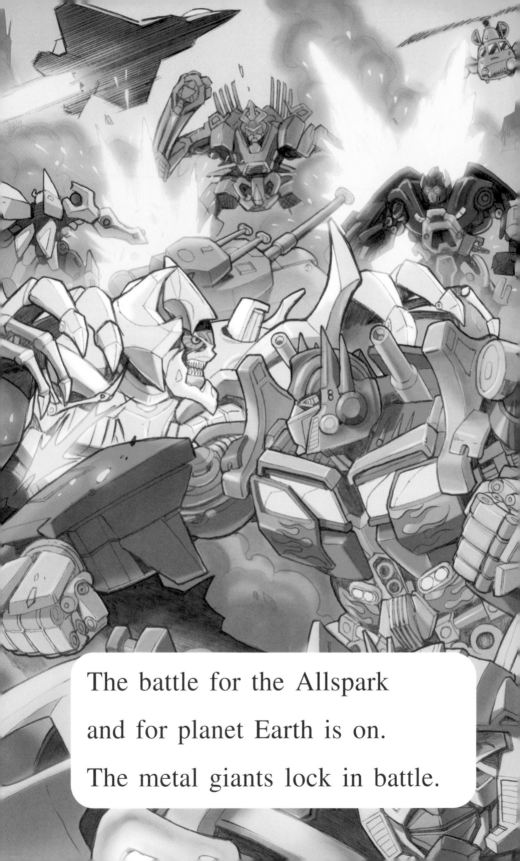

The battle for the Allspark
and for planet Earth is on.
The metal giants lock in battle.

Megatron takes a hit!

The Decepticons lose this battle!

They flee the planet.

For now the Earth is safe.

TRANSFORMERS
REVENGE OF THE FALLEN

I Am Optimus Prime

I Am Optimus Prime

Adapted by Jennifer Frantz

Illustrations by Guido Guidi

Based on the Screenplay by
Ehren Kruger & Alex Kurtzman & Roberto Orci

Optimus Prime is the brave leader
of the Autobots.
They are robots in disguise!

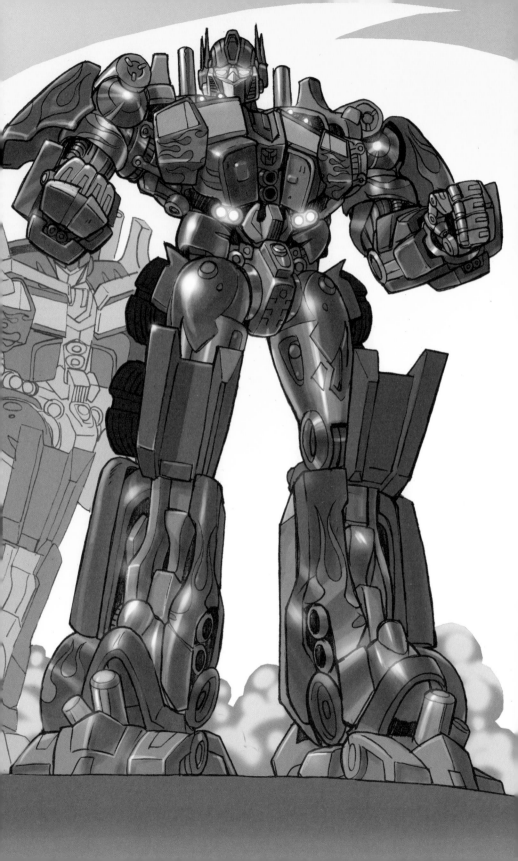

Optimus is not just any 'bot.

He is the last of the great Primes,

a line of noble robots.

They come from

the planet Cybertron.

Like all true Primes,

Optimus fights for what is right.

Here on planet Earth,

Optimus Prime

is a friend to humans.

Side by side,

humans and Autobots battled Megatron

and his evil Decepticons.

Now Earth has a new threat.

And Optimus Prime has a new enemy.

The enemy's name is The Fallen.

The Fallen is even more evil
and powerful than Megatron.
He feeds on energy,
growing stronger and stronger.
The Fallen wants to absorb
the sun's energy
and destroy planet Earth.

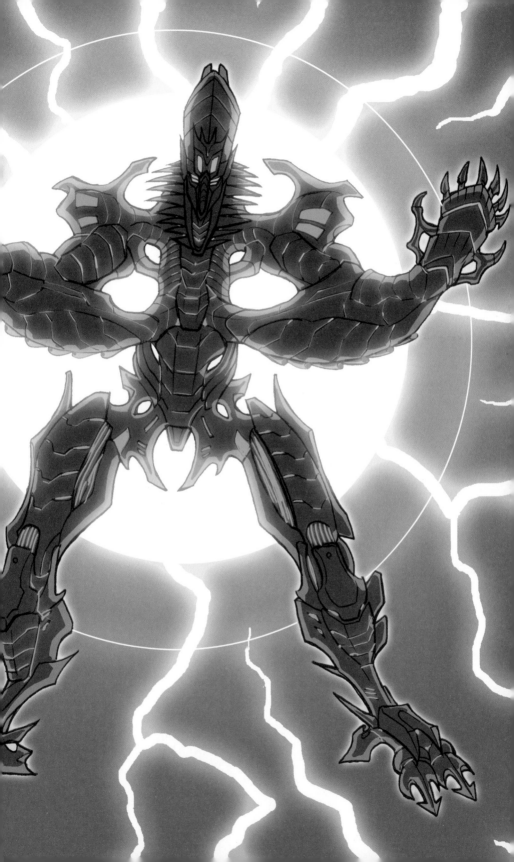

Optimus Prime must
stop The Fallen.
But he is not alone!

The brave Autobots are ready to do whatever their leader asks.

Look out, Decepticons!
The Twins might look little
but they are double trouble.

Ironhide and Optimus Prime

make a great team.

Together they defeat the evil Demolisher.

Bumblebee is a loyal 'bot.

He will go anywhere

to help a friend.

Sideswipe is a fearless fighter.

He will do anything

for Optimus Prime.

The battle is on!
The Autobots face off
against the Decepticons.

Optimus Prime is ready to rumble!

Bumblebee blasts
a bulldozing Decepticon!
Bumblebee is small and fast.

Bumblebee has never fought better.

He wins this battle!

The Twins take on
the deadly Devastator.

This giant 'bot
is bad news!

In the end,

Optimus Prime sends The Fallen

screaming into space.

The sun is saved.

Optimus made the Earth safe
from Decepticons.
At least, for now.

ROBOT ROLL CALL
Story by Jennifer Frantz

The Autobots are strangers in a strange, new land—planet Earth.

In this new world,

the Autobots try their best

to blend in.

Sometimes it is easy to stay off the radar.

But sometimes the Autobots have

a hard time keeping a low profile.

All the Autobots

look up to **Optimus Prime**.

He is a brave leader

and a true friend.

When one of his friends

is in trouble,

his trusty tools

come to the rescue.

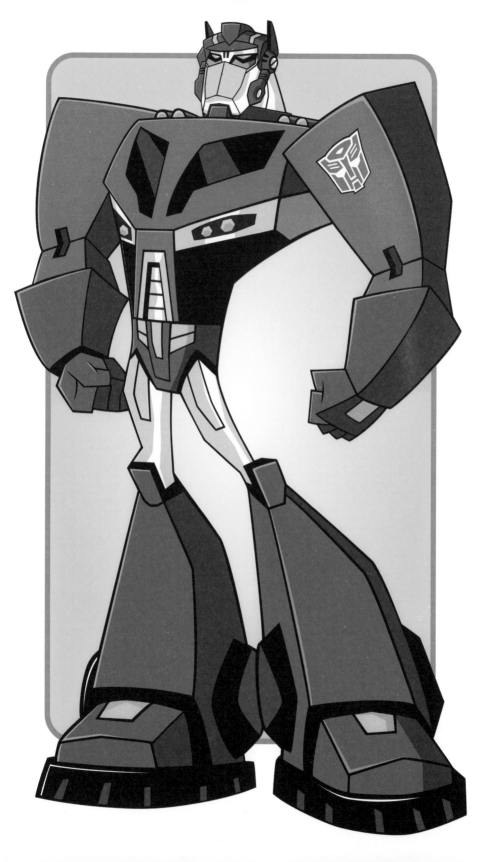

Bulkhead is a gentle giant.

But the bad guys should watch out!

This big bot can bust things up.

Bumblebee thinks Earth

is the place to be.

It's fast, fun,

and flashy.

Just like he is!

Bumblebee is always ready for action.

His stinger blasts

can stun anything

in his path.

Prowl loves to look at nature.

And just like a cat,

he is always

ready to pounce.

With his super senses and sneaky moves,

Prowl can creep up on any enemy.

Ratchet is one

of the oldest Autobots.

He can be gruff and tough,

but is always there

for a bot in need.

Ratchet uses

his magnetic powers

and medical skills

to patch up fallen friends.

Sari Sumdac loves
to hang out with her
Autobot pals.
And her special energy key
can heal bots hurt in battle.

Sari's dad, **Isaac**, is a robot scientist. Busy and curious, his mind is always on his work.

The Autobots are not the only ones
new to planet Earth.

Megatron is the leader
of the Decepticons.
He wants
to control the Allspark,
the source of all energy.
First he must
stop the Autobots,
and anyone else
who stands in his way.

Starscream is fast,

fierce, and full of lies.

No one can trust him,

not even the other

Decepticons.

He streaks

onto the scene

and sends out

a supersonic scream.

Blackarachnia
is loyal to
only one
Decepticon—
herself.

Any bot who falls under her spell
will get stung with her venom.

A sly robot hunter,

Lockdown will work

for anyone,

if the price is right.

No bot wants

to get snared

in his deadly net.

Lugnut is a supersized threat!
This bomb-blasting brute
is as wild as a pit bull.

And he will fight to the end

for his master, Megatron.

The Autobots and the Decepticons
are powerful forces.

No one knows what will happen when they face off.

Planet Earth

will never be the same!

Rise of the Decepticons

TRANSFORMERS
REVENGE OF THE FALLEN

Rise of the Decepticons

Adapted by Jennifer Frantz

Illustrations by Marcelo Matere

Based on the Screenplay by
Ehren Kruger & Alex Kurtzman & Roberto Orci

The evil Megatron lost
his last battle
with Optimus Prime,
the leader of the Autobots.

Megatron is the leader
of the Decepticons.
Decepticons and Autobots
are sworn enemies.

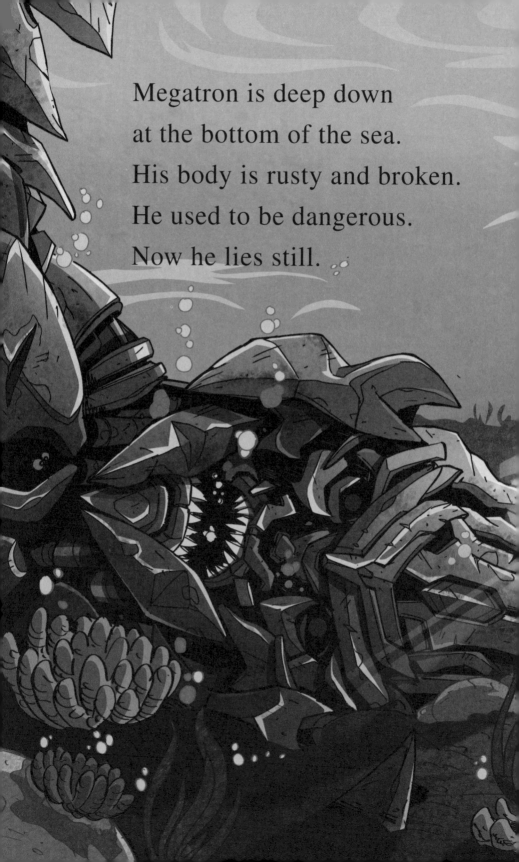

Megatron is deep down
at the bottom of the sea.
His body is rusty and broken.
He used to be dangerous.
Now he lies still.

Humans don't want Megatron
to rise up again.
The Navy watches over him
with submarines.

Megatron's Decepticon forces
want to get their leader back.
Soundwave hacks into
the Navy computers.

Soundwave finds all the top secret
information he needs.
Now the Decepticons can make a plan.

The Decepticons must get
the Allspark shard.
It was the source of
Megatron's energy.

The shard is in a locked vault.
Ravage outsmarts the humans.
He gets the shard!

Now that they have the shard, the Decepticons are ready to go to their leader.

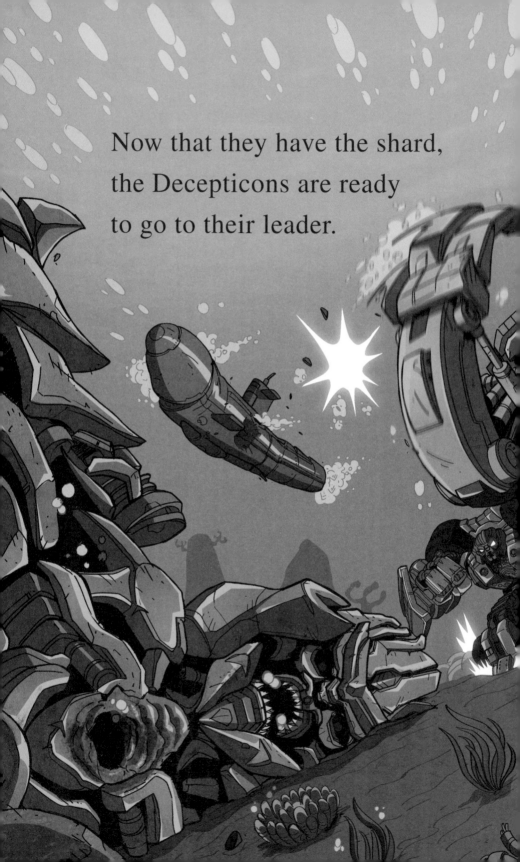

The Decepticons get past
the submarines.
The evil 'bots find Megatron.

The Doctor is a nimble 'bot.
Using his jointed arms,
the Doctor puts the shard
into Megatron.

Megatron bursts to life!
He's back and he's bad.

Now the good guys
have to watch out.
The battle for Earth
has never been harder.

Megatron is not alone.

His Decepticon army is by his side.

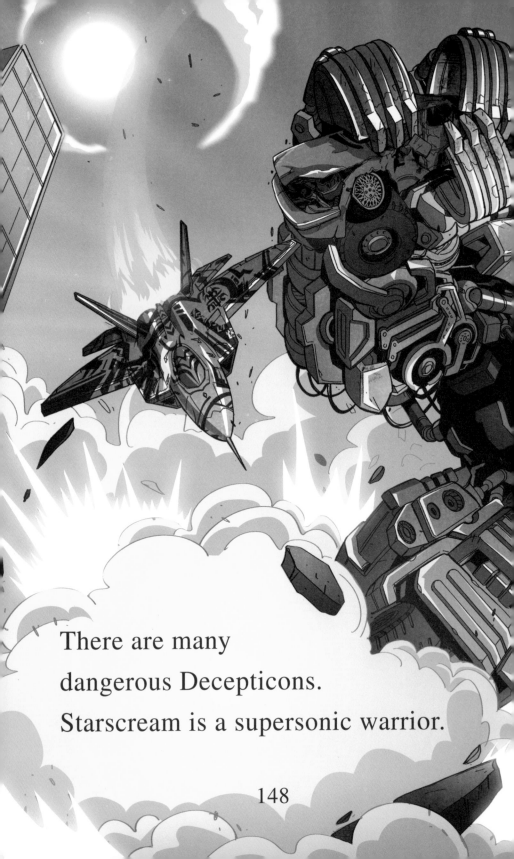

There are many
dangerous Decepticons.
Starscream is a supersonic warrior.

Devastator is one MEGA-bot!
He is a scary foe.

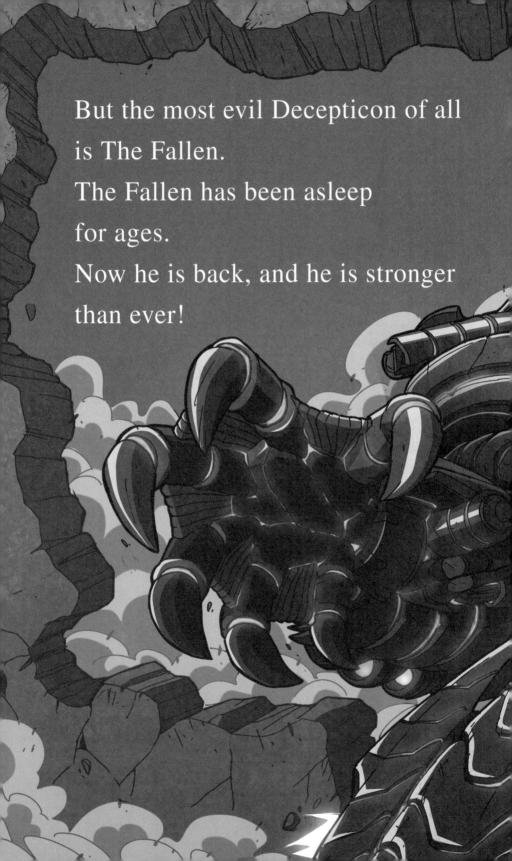

But the most evil Decepticon of all
is The Fallen.
The Fallen has been asleep
for ages.
Now he is back, and he is stronger
than ever!

The Autobots
and their human friends
prepare for one hard fight.

Luckily, the Autobots have
two secret weapons.
Wheels and Jetfire are Decepticons
who changed sides.

Now they fight for good
with Optimus Prime
and the Autobots.

Wheels is small,
but he is as brave
as the biggest 'bot.

Jetfire is old,
but he is still very powerful.
He is also very wise.

Can the Autobots beat
the Decepticons once again?

Or will Megatron and The Fallen
be too powerful?

Only one thing is sure:
Optimus Prime and his Autobots
will never give up!

THE DECEPTICONS INVADE!

Adapted by Olivia London
Illustrations by Carlo Lo Raso

Based on the episode *Lost and Found*,
written by Rich Fogel

On a sunny day in Detroit,
Sari was playing street hockey
with her friends the Autobots.
Suddenly, her key began to glow.
Danger was near!

Two fireballs zoomed across the sky
and crashed.

The fireballs were Decepticons
named Lugnut and Blitzwing!

They were looking for their leader.

"Where is Megatron?" Lugnut said.

The Autobots knew the Decepticons
were going to cause trouble.
The Autobots had to stop them!

"Autobots, roll out!"

ordered their leader, Optimus Prime.

"Looking for us?" Optimus called

to the Decepticons.

Ratchet blocked Decepticon missiles

with his shield.

Lugnut threw a truck at Optimus,
but Optimus sliced it in half!
"I think we got their attention,"
said Optimus.

Lugnut was angry.

He smashed his fist into the ground, making a big explosion.

KABOOM!

The blast knocked down the Autobots.

Then the Decepticons disappeared.

Megatron watched Lugnut and Blitzwing on a video screen. He knew this was his chance to get the AllSpark!

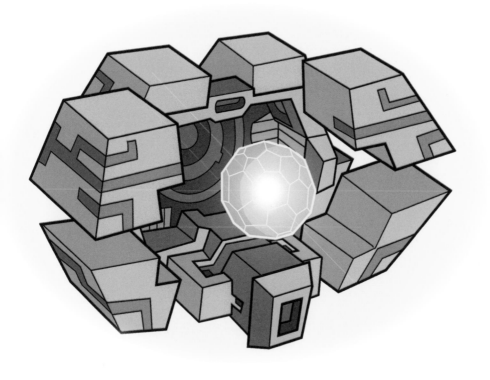

The AllSpark was the source

of all Transformer life.

Megatron needed its power

to defeat the Autobots.

He would make Lugnut and Blitzwing

bring it to him.

The Autobots had survived this battle, but they knew there would be more. "We cannot risk causing danger to this planet," said Optimus.

They would have to take the AllSpark
and leave Earth.

The AllSpark was in
the Autobots' broken ship.
The ship lay at the bottom of a lake.
Only the power from Sari's key
could fix the ship.

But Megatron had a different plan.

He sent Lugnut an image of the key.

"Follow it to the AllSpark," he said.

"Then bring the AllSpark to me!"

At the lake, Ratchet transformed

into an ambulance.

Just then, Sari's key started to glow.

The Decepticons were near!

Lugnut and Blitzwing fired.

"Go to the ship,"

Optimus told Ratchet and Sari.

"We will stay and fight them."

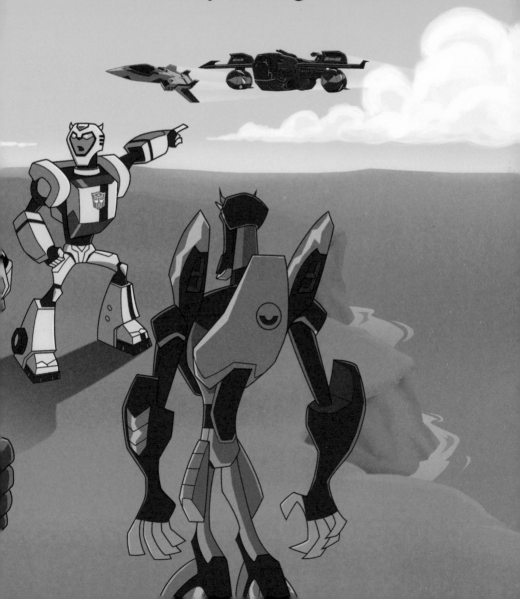

The battle moved underwater.

The Autobots were clever fighters.

Optimus spun his wheels

and made a thick cloud of sand.

Lugnut could not see, and he fired

at Blitzwing by mistake!

While the others were fighting,
Ratchet and Sari found the ship.
Ratchet was so happy to see it.

But Sari was sad.

She did not want her friends to go.

Ratchet knew how Sari felt.

"I will miss you, too," he told her.

"But we must stop the Decepticons!"

Sari knew he was right.

She promised to help fix the ship.

Ratchet told Sari that the ship
had weapons that did not work.

"If we can fix them, we can beat the Decepticons," he said.

They soon came up with a plan.

Ratchet called Optimus
over their radio connection.
"Optimus, draw the Decepticons
to the ship!" he cried.

When the Decepticons were close,

Ratchet fired a powerful blast.

It knocked out Lugnut and Blitzwing.

The Autobots had won!

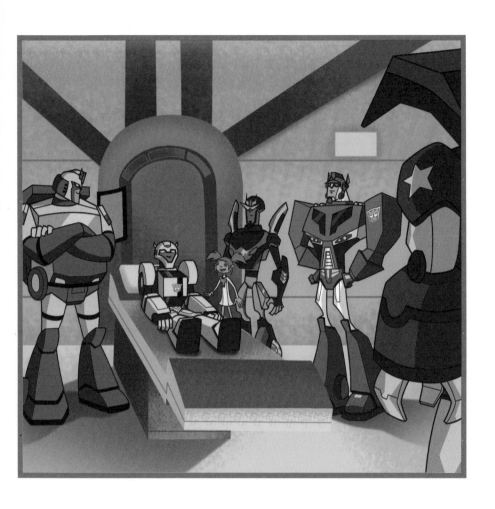

The Autobots and the AllSpark
were safe for now.
"Tomorrow we will finish
fixing your ship," Sari told them.

"No rush," said Ratchet.
"We might stick around
for a very long time!"